Bad News

"Oh no," Mom said softly. I don't believe this."

"What?" I said.

Mom groaned. "It's Jessica's pageant," she explained. "You remember—the Little Miss Apple Blossom pageant that she wants to be in so much."

"Yeah, I remember," I said. "What about it?"

"It's the same night as your play!" Mom said. I felt my stomach dive to the bottom of my sneakers.

"But that doesn't make any difference, does it, Mom?" I asked anxiously. "I mean, Jessica's already been in a million pageants, right? You'll still come to my play, won't you? Jessica can drop out of this one pageant, can't she, Mom? Mom?"

"Oh, Jill, honey, I wish it were that easy, I really do. But I've invested too much in this for Jessica to drop out. Oh, and I really want to see your play!"

I couldn't believe what I was hearing. "*What?*" I yelled. "You can't mean you're not coming?"

Books by Constance Hiser

Critter Sitters
Dog on Third Base
Ghosts in Fourth Grade
No Bean Sprouts, Please!
Sixth-Grade Star

Available from MINSTREL Books

Sixth-Grade STAR

Constance Hiser

A MINSTREL® BOOK

Published by POCKET BOOKS
New York   London   Toronto   Sydney   Tokyo   Singapore

A Minstrel Book published by
POCKET BOOKS, a division of Simon & Schuster Inc.
1230 Avenue of the Americas, New York, NY 10020

Copyright © 1992 by Constance Hiser

Published by arrangement with Holiday House, Inc.

ISBN: 0-671-87116-1

First Minstrel Books printing December 1996

10 9 8 7 6 5 4 3 2 1

A MINSTREL BOOK and colophon are registered trademarks of Simon & Schuster Inc.

Cover art by Carla D'Aguanno

Printed in the U.S.A.

*For my mother and father,
who never played favorites*

Contents

CHAPTER ONE

My Roommate, Miss America

"I swear, it gets worse in here every day!" I shoved the little mountain of junk on my bed, and it fell to the floor with a crash. "It's bad enough that I have to share a room with the little princess. Wouldn't you think she could at least keep her stuff off my bed?"

"Oh, I think it's all kind of interesting," said Wendy Ryan, my very best friend in the whole wide world. She picked up a rhinestone crown from the floor and twirled it around on one finger. "I wish *I* could win a beauty contest." She looked around the room at the trophies, certificates, and rhine-stone crowns that were everywhere—not just on my bed, but on my sister's bed, both bedside tables, and the desks that we could never use for doing homework, because Jessica piled stuff on both of them.

Wendy opened my closet and stood in front of the long mirror that hung on the inside of the door. Then she jammed the crown down over her red hair and struck a glamorous pose. "It'll never happen," she sighed, frowning at her reflection.

I couldn't really disagree with her. Wendy looked silly in her jeans and sweatshirt with her hair coming out of her ponytail under the crown. Even dressed up for a party, Wendy didn't have the kind of looks that would get you very far in a beauty contest—it took someone like my little sister Jessica for that. But I'd rather have Wendy for a friend than all the beauty queens in the world. At least she'd never pile her scrapbooks and ribbons in the middle of my bed!

"Believe me," I told her, "you don't want to have anything to do with those pageants Jessica's always entering. They're just plain dumb. And they're not near as much fun as they're cracked up to be."

Wendy looked at me in the mirror as she slowly took the sparkling crown from her head and carefully placed it on the bedside table. "Weren't you in a contest once?" she asked. "Wasn't it exciting?"

I flopped down on my back in the middle of my bed. "That's not the word I'd pick for it," I said. "In the first place, it—"

Wendy and I nearly jumped out of our skins as the bedroom door flew open and crashed against the wall.

"Hi, guys!" My little sister Jessica stood in the doorway, her perfect teeth gleaming in a smile that brought out that adorable dimple in her left cheek—the one that always makes me want to puke. "What are you doing?"

"We're *trying* to study for a history test," I informed her. Then I took another look at her and frowned. "What kind of getup is that supposed to be?"

"Oh, you mean my new costume?" She twirled around, making her full skirt bell out. "It's for the talent part of the Maple

Sugar Princess contest on Saturday. Do you like it?"

"Who wouldn't?" I asked. I was being sarcastic, but Jessica didn't seem to catch on. "What are you supposed to be, anyway?"

"I'm a Swiss mountain girl—you know, like Heidi, and—"

"Terrific," I interrupted, making a face at Wendy to stop her from asking questions. Give Jessica an inch of encouragement and she'll talk all night about her stupid beauty pageants. "Well, Jess, sorry to be rude, but we have this big test, so—"

"That's just the cutest costume I ever saw!" I glared at Wendy as she piped up. "All those petticoats, and ribbons, and lace—and what's that in your arms? A toy goat? What a fantastic idea! You're going to look like something out of a magazine!"

Jessica beamed at her. "Hey, thanks, Wendy! I'm going to do a yodeling song, like this—'Yodel-lay-dee-hooo!' " Jessica made a noise that sounded like a howling dog, as she adjusted the little wreath of white flowers that lay on top of her oh-so-perfect black curls. "You want to hear the rest?"

"No!" I exclaimed, but Jessica had already

popped a cassette into the player and was dancing around our bedroom in a swirl of red lacy skirts, that ridiculous stuffed goat in her arms.

" 'Yodel-lay-dee-hoo, yodel-lay-dee-hee, yodel—' " she sang in a chirpy voice, flashing her adorable smile. It made me sick. Wendy was eating it all up, though, perched on the side of Jessica's bed with a star-struck expression in her eyes. Wendy always was a lot more impressed with Jessica than I was.

" 'Away up in the mountains, high in the snowcapped mountains—' " Jessica struck a precious pose, lifting her face up toward the bedroom ceiling as if she were feeling mountain sunlight on her cute little face. It would probably melt the judges' hearts, but it only gave me heartburn.

" 'Where every day is happy, bright, and free—' " Opening those big, violet-blue eyes as wide as they'd go, Jessica gave a little skip, and the bells sewed to her petticoats rang.

"Oh, please!" I moaned, rolling over and burying my head in my pillow. "We have a test tomorrow, remember?" But I knew we'd have to listen to the whole sickening routine, right to the last gaggy note.

Sixth grade was hard enough, I thought, as my sister cooed and twirled while Wendy *ooh*ed and *aah*ed. Was it too much to ask for a little *study time*, for pete's sake?

" 'Way up in the mountains, the sunlit, peaceful mountains—' " Jessica caroled, while I pulled the pillow down over my ears. If I flunked that history test tomorrow, I knew who I could blame. For all the good it would do.

"But, Mom!" I heard that whiny sound sneaking into my voice. I hated that—twelve was much too old for whining—but I couldn't stop myself. "But, Mom, didn't you even hear what I *said*? She had her dumb old scrapbooks and crowns and ribbons and stuff all over *my* bed. I couldn't even sit down! And then, when Wendy and I were trying to study, she had to come barging in with her nauseating song and her stupid costume."

"It's not stupid!" Jessica kicked my leg under the table and stuck out her tongue at me. I wished those pageant judges could see her sometime with milk all over her tongue. Gross. "Jill's just jealous, Mom, because she couldn't win a contest if her life depended on it."

"I am *not* jealous!" I yelled, jumping up from my chair. I was seriously considering yanking every one of her darling curls right out of her head. "I wouldn't enter one of those dumb contests if you paid me to! They're for people who are too stuck-up and conceited to do anything important, like study for their exams! And besides, Jessica Sue Armstrong—"

"Girls!" My mother set her coffee cup down in its saucer so hard that it rattled. "Girls, you stop it this second! Good grief, is it too much to ask for a little peace and quiet at home after working all day long? Do you *want* to drive me crazy?"

I stared down at my plate full of meat loaf and peas and mashed potatoes, feeling guilty, the way Mom could always make me feel. Ever since my dad died of cancer, when Jessica was just a baby, Mom had had to work pretty hard. It was more than just her job, downtown at the doctor's office. She had to manage everything here at home, too.

"No, Mom," I muttered, stabbing a pea with my fork. "Sorry, Mom."

Out of the corner of my eye, I saw Jessica flash one of those iceberg-melting smiles of hers. "I'm sorry, too, Mama," she said sweetly.

Mom rubbed at her forehead, and I wondered if she was getting one of her headaches. "That's better," she said. She sounded tired. "Jessica, honey, you try to keep things on your own side of the room, will you, please? And come downstairs to practice when Jill is studying." Then she looked at me. "And Jill, it wouldn't hurt for you to take an interest in your little sister. You ought to be *proud* of her. How many girls do you know who've already won seven beauty pageants by the time they're nine years old?"

Jessica smirked at me from across the table, and I had to twist my hand up in the edge of the tablecloth to keep from leaning forward and smacking her.

"Not many, Mom," I said. "Jessica's one of a kind, all right."

"And so are you," Mom said, patting my hand. "I'm proud of *both* my girls, you know. You're well on your way to making straight A's this semester. And if Jessica keeps winning pageants at this rate, she'll be a real *star* someday! Why, she could even be *Miss America*."

Jessica and Mom now wore identical dreamy expressions. I sighed. I had seen those looks before, and I knew I was in for a solid hour of daydreaming.

"Atlantic City," my mother said softly. "All those cameras flashing, and those beautiful dresses, and the flowers, lots of flowers."

"Reporters," Jessica chimed in. She looked just the way she used to look when we were both little and talked about Santa Claus. "That big, sparkly crown, and dancers, and someone singing 'There She Is, Miss America,' while I walk down the runway in a glittery gold dress . . ."

That was all I could take. "Excuse me," I said, scraping the last mouthful of meat loaf from my plate. "I have a test to study for. Jess, your turn to do the dishes."

That brought her home from Atlantic City in a hurry. "But I have to practice!" she wailed. "The Maple Sugar Princess pageant is Saturday. I don't have *time* to do the dishes!"

I froze in the kitchen doorway. "Oh, give

me a break, Jessica—" I began, but Mom interrupted quickly.

"Jill, you wash, and Jessica, you dry," she said. "That way it won't take either of you very long. You'd better get a move on, Jessica—you have to try on your new formal so I can hem it. And Jill, you should have plenty of time to study once the dishes are done."

"Not fair," I mumbled under my breath. I clenched my hands into fists and gritted my teeth. Mom's tired, I reminded myself over and over, as I clattered the dishes into a stack beside the kitchen sink. Mom's tired. Don't lose your temper.

But it was hard. And it didn't get any easier when, the minute the last dish was dried, I heard the cassette player blaring in the living room. " 'Yodel-lay-dee-hooooo—' " Jessica warbled.

It wouldn't take much to make me really *hate* that song, I decided, banging cups and plates and saucers onto the shelves and slamming the cabinet doors—hard.

CHAPTER TWO

All You Gotta Do Is Try

"Jill! Did you *see*?" Wendy's red hair practically crackled around her face as she ran to meet me at school the next morning. I had never seen her look more excited.

I yawned—I had been up late studying. "See what?" I asked sleepily. "Did Tim Barton fall off the jungle gym again?"

"No!" She shook her head, making her ponytail whip back and forth. "Better than that! Miss Carnine just posted the list for tryouts for the spring play!"

"So?" I asked, taking off my jacket and

hanging it on its hook in the back of the sixth-grade classroom. "What's so exciting about that? The sixth grade does a play every year."

"But this is the first time *we've* been in the sixth grade!" Wendy pointed out. "And, oh, Jill, wait till you hear—this year we're going to do *The Wizard of Oz*! Witches and Munchkins and wizards and the whole thing. I bet it'll be the best play any sixth grade has ever done."

Now I couldn't help feeling a little excited, too. Ever since I was a kid, *The Wizard of Oz* has been one of my favorite movies. We'd bought the video as soon as it came out, and I must have watched it a million times. I practically had the whole thing memorized! I could still remember getting in trouble when I was six for coloring my best white shoes with a red felt-tip marker so I could pretend they were Dorothy's ruby slippers.

"*The Wizard of Oz*?" I said. "Wow, Wendy, that really is terrific. I don't think the sixth grade has ever put on a play like that before, with music and dancing and everything."

"That's what I was *saying*!" Wendy said impatiently. "And there are enough parts for everyone, too—the ones who don't want to try out for a big part can be Munchkins."

"That would be good enough for me," I said. I put my lunch box on the shelf under the aquarium, and dropped my book bag on top of my desk. "I don't want a real part—I just think it will be fun to be in something that special."

Wendy frowned. "What do you mean, you don't want a real part?" she asked. "*The Wizard of Oz*—think about it, Jill! It's your all-time favorite. Don't you remember the way you always played Dorothy when we used to act it out in your backyard? You did a great job, too. You have to try out for something!"

"I don't know," I said. "Jessica's the star in our family. One is probably enough."

"That's *another* reason for you to try out," Wendy insisted. "Why should Jessica hog all the glory? You're every bit as pretty as she is—well, practically, anyway. And you're a much better singer. Don't you think it's time she finds out she's not the only talented person in your family?"

Sometimes Wendy has a way of putting things that makes a lot of sense.

"I hadn't thought about that," I said slowly. "I guess—I guess you might be right."

"Think how proud your mom would be," Wendy coaxed.

That was all she had to say. "Where is that tryout list?" I asked, standing up and heading for the classroom door.

Wendy grinned. "In the hall, next to the cafeteria," she said. "You mean you're going to do it, Jill? You're going to try out for Dorothy?"

I stared at her. *Dorothy?* I said. "You've got to be kidding! I wouldn't have a chance. Besides, I'd be too nervous. No, but there must be something else I could try out for— something a little more my speed. Like the Good Witch, maybe—she has one or two good scenes. Or maybe Auntie Em. What about you?"

"I'm going to sign up for the Munchkins and set painting," Wendy answered. "I think it would be fun to paint all those scenes of Oz. But I still think you'd make a great Dorothy. Anyway, the important thing is that you're going to try out for *something*."

"Absolutely," I answered, looking at the

tryout list to see who had signed up so far. Paige Underwood wanted to be Dorothy, I noticed—well, that didn't surprise me. A couple of other girls were trying out too, but they didn't have a chance. I wouldn't have been much competition either—besides being the prettiest girl in sixth grade, Paige could sing and dance like a Broadway star. If there's one thing I know, it's when I'm outclassed.

Pulling the cap off my ballpoint pen, I wrote my name beside both the *Good Witch* and *Auntie Em*. People like Paige Underwood wouldn't bother with parts like those, so I figured I stood a chance.

"You have a whole week to practice, too," Wendy pointed out. "Tryouts won't be till next Thursday. Oh, yeah—you're supposed to get a script from Miss Carnine, so you can study your part before the tryouts. And I'd like to talk to her about the set crew."

"So what are we waiting for?" I asked. "Let's go!"

The two of us headed for the music room.

Hollywood, here I come! I thought, joining the line of sixth graders waiting for Miss Carnine, the music teacher. Who would want to be Little Miss Cabbagehead, when they had a chance to be Auntie Em?

"Mom!" I yelled, for what must have been the fortieth time that evening. "Make Jessica turn this dumb cassette player off! How can I learn my lines if she's yodeling in my ear all the time?"

"I am not!" Jessica yelled back. "This is only the fourth time I've sung this song tonight, Jill, and you know it! Besides, I've got to practice—it's only two more days until the pageant."

I picked up one of my tennis shoes and threw it at her.

"So?" I screamed. "So since when are you the only person in this whole house who has things to do, Jessica Sue Armstrong? *Important* things. I have a play to try out for."

"Who cares about some dumb old play?" She threw my tennis shoe right back at me. "It's just a school play, anyway, not a Hollywood movie, for pete's sake! Nobody would even go to *see* those plays if their own kids weren't in them!"

"Is that so?" I snapped. "And I suppose

that thousands and thousands of people are going to be lined up to watch you sing that dumb song in the Miss Vanilla Bean contest on Saturday?"

"It's the Maple Sugar Princess contest, you big dummy!" she shrieked. "And you'll notice that the Miss America pageant is on TV every year, but when's the last time you ever saw a play on television? That proves that beauty contests are more important than stupid school plays!"

"*The Wizard of Oz*," I reminded her, "is on TV every year, too. And you know you've seen the video. But I guess you're too stuck-up to realize it's really a *play*. You think there's nothing more to life than formals and crowns and prancing around a stage in silly costumes, and—"

"Jill! Jessica! That's *enough*!" Mom was standing in the bedroom doorway, and she looked mad. "What's the matter with you two? Can't you be together for five minutes without trying to rip each other's heads off? Honestly, I don't know what to do with the two of you!"

Jessica and I glared at each other. Neither one of us was going to back down an inch.

"She started it," I muttered, even though I knew I was probably just going to make Mom angrier than she already was. "I was in here trying to study my lines, and she barged in and—"

"I did *not* barge in!" Jessica's cheeks were red, and her eyes were snapping. "This is my room, too, Jill Armstrong, and I can come in any time I—"

"Stop!" my mom yelled. "You two stop this *right now*, do you hear me? I can see that if I'm going to get any quiet at all this evening, I'm going to have to separate the two of you. Jill, you stay in here and study your script. Jessica, bring the cassette player and come downstairs. You can practice your song in the den. Now, does that suit everyone?"

"Suits me fine!" Jessica snarled, picking up the cassette player. "I can't sing in a room where nobody appreciates me!"

"That means you can't sing anywhere!" I couldn't resist yelling it at her as she left the room, but the look my mother gave me made me wish I hadn't. Then she was gone, shutting the door behind her, and I had the whole room to myself. At last. All the peace and quiet I needed to learn my lines.

Somehow I didn't feel great about it, though. Why did Jessica have to make so much trouble for me, whatever I tried to do? Come to think of it, why did there even have to *be* a Jessica? I couldn't remember it well, but I was pretty sure I had managed fine before she had been born. And I probably could have kept right on managing.

"I don't know, Wendy," I whispered nervously on the day of the tryouts. "I don't know if I can do it."

"Relax, Jill," she whispered back.

I shuddered as I looked up at the stage, where Paige Underwood was doing a terrific job singing Dorothy's big song from the first act. "Getting up in front of all these people! Oh, I'm going to make an idiot of myself! I can't go up there!"

"Not even as Auntie Em?" she begged. "She doesn't have to sing anything. And you know all those lines perfectly, Jill, I know you do. I bet you could say them in your sleep."

"I don't," I moaned. "I'll probably forget every word the minute I'm up there."

"What's the big deal, Jill?" Wendy asked. "You know everyone in this room. What do you think we're going to do, throw bricks at you?"

"Everyone will laugh," I whispered nervously. "No one ever laughs at Jessica."

Wendy looked at me until I felt like hiding behind my script. That's the only bad thing about having a friend like Wendy—sometimes she knows me better than I know myself, and there's no use trying to hide anything from her.

"That's what this whole thing is about, isn't it?" she asked. "You don't think you're as good as Jessica at anything."

"I do!" I shot back. "I make better grades than she does. And she couldn't hit a baseball if her life depended on it. It's just when it comes to getting up on a stage in front of a lot of people—"

"But you can do it," Wendy urged as Paige hit the beautiful high note to end her song. The whole auditorium full of sixth graders broke into loud applause. Paige smiled and took a little bow as if she already had the part and it was the night of the play. I could never be like that, I thought gloomily.

But I didn't have long to worry about it, because just then Miss Carnine stepped up to the front of the stage. "Very nice, Paige!" she said brightly. "Next we'll have—let's see—oh, yes, *Jill!* Jill Armstrong! Where are you, Jill?"

There was an awful, high-pitched ringing in my ears, so loud I couldn't even hear all the kids whispering and laughing as I got up and stumbled toward the front. I could feel my face get hot as I bumbled up the stairs and onstage, where Miss Carnine stood waiting with a big smile on her face.

"Anytime you're ready, Jill," she said, taking her seat in a folding chair. "You're trying out for Auntie Em, aren't you? Why don't we start with this scene on page three, the one where you're calling Dorothy?"

I stood there on rubbery legs, looking out at a sea of faces that seemed to blur and swim together. Why had I never noticed how many people there were in sixth grade?

"Jill?" Miss Carnine said. "Jill, you can start anytime, dear."

I opened my mouth. Frantically, I tried to

make those first words come out—but nothing happened. I couldn't even get a croak through my lips.

"Jill?" Miss Carnine said again.

And I knew I couldn't do it. Feeling my eyes fill up with tears, I whirled and clomped back down the stairs and ran through the crowd of whispering kids. I didn't stop until I'd gotten to the hall, where I slouched against the wall, my heart hammering and my stomach doing somersaults.

What's the matter with me? I wondered miserably. Why can't I do anything right?

Behind me, I heard the whooshing sound of the auditorium door opening. A second later, I felt a hand come down gently on my shoulder, and I looked up into the face of Miss Carnine.

"Jill?" she asked softly. "Jill, what happened in there?"

I shook my head while the tears streamed down my face. "I don't know, Miss Carnine," I sobbed. "I thought I could do it, I really did. But I saw everyone looking at me, and I—I guess I got scared."

She smiled. "Don't you know that most of the kids up there are scared out of their wits?" she asked. "Why, that's part of performing, Jill. The biggest stars in Hollywood get nervous sometimes."

"I'm not a star," I said, in such a little voice I wasn't even sure she could hear me. "Paige Underwood, she's a star. My sister Jessica, she's a star. Not me."

Miss Carnine put one arm around my shoulders. "Jill," she said, "I can't make you go back in there. I'm not even going to try. But I think you're the one who'll be sorriest if you don't, because for the rest of your life you'll wonder if you could have done it—if maybe, just maybe, there's a little bit of star in you, after all."

I sighed. "I know," I said. "And I really want to be in the play. Not even in a big part. Auntie Em would be good enough. But I'm not sure I can even do that."

"So you're going to give up without even trying?" Miss Carnine said. I thought she sounded disappointed. "I never thought you were a quitter, Jill."

That hurt! Surprised, I looked up at her through my tears. "I'm not!" I said. "I'm *not* a quitter, Miss Carnine!"

She smiled. "Then show me," she said.

"Just get up on that stage and read a few lines. That's all I ask."

Now how can I get out of *this* one? I thought. I didn't see a way, so I made myself smile. "Okay," I said. "I'll do it. But just a few lines. And—and, Miss Carnine, if—if I really blow it, I'll understand if you don't give me any part at all. Honest, I will."

"Let's see how you do first." She laughed, and then she pushed the auditorium door open and marched me back in there before I could change my mind.

Walking past all those staring sixth graders was one of the hardest things I ever had to do. I was so embarrassed, I wished the floor would open and suck me down into some other dimension. But I kept on walking, feeling numb, listening to the way the blood pounded in my ears.

The stage seemed a hundred feet high, but somehow I made it up those steps and found myself standing center stage again, with what seemed like thousands of eyes glued to me. I can't do it! I thought, beginning to panic again. I'm sorry, Miss Carnine, I just can't do it! I turned around to tell her that, but she winked and gave me a thumbs-up signal.

This time, somehow, when I opened my mouth, words actually came out. And even before I was through, I could feel a big grin spreading across my face. This time, I knew, I was fine, just fine.

Maybe Jessica wasn't the only star in the Armstrong family!

CHAPTER THREE

Oz, Here I Come!

"Yay, Jill!" Wendy jumped up and down and cheered right there in the middle of the hallway.

I looked at the list Miss Carnine had posted. I could hardly believe what I saw. Right there by the words *Auntie Em* was my very own name, JILL ARMSTRONG, in big capital letters!

I had done it—I had gotten a part in the sixth-grade play.

"Wow!" Wendy said. "You're practically

Princess of May, Queen of the Frost, Little Miss Snowflake—"

"I know all that," Wendy interrupted impatiently. "I practically live at your house, remember? Anyway, I want to hear about you, not Jess and your mom."

"Well," I went on, "when I was about seven, I decided to go along with them. I asked Mom if I could enter a pageant they were having that spring—Junior Miss Azalea, I think it was called."

"Yeah!" Wendy exclaimed. "I knew you'd been in a contest once. Did you win?"

I snorted. "Give me a break, Wendy. I wasn't even thinking about winning. All I wanted was to get my share of the attention for a change."

"And did it work?" Wendy asked.

"And how!" I answered. "You would have thought I'd been elected President, the way Mom carried on. She made me get a perm—my hair looked like a brown Brillo pad. She even made me practice walking with a book on top of my head. And she painted this awful-tasting gunk on my fingernails so I'd stop biting them. I got a long dress, too—I remember that it was blue, with a million ruffles on it. I *hated* that dress. And that wasn't even the worst part."

"Oh, come on," Wendy laughed. "It couldn't have been *that* bad."

"Wanna bet?" I said. "There's always a talent competition in those pageants, remember? I wanted to play a song on the piano, but Mom said that wasn't flashy enough. She made me a red-checked dress with a great big skirt and five or six petticoats underneath to make it stand out. Then she painted little freckles all over my face with her eyeliner brush."

Wendy couldn't quite keep herself from laughing.

"Then," I went on, "Mom found a dumb-looking stuffed chicken in the toy store and made me hold it under one arm. She dug up a cassette of some barfy country-western song, I don't remember what, and I had to prance around and sing and pretend to be a cute little country girl. I still remember the way my stomach felt while I was standing there in the middle of the stage with that stupid chicken, waiting for the curtain to go up. I never felt so scared in my whole life."

"Poor Jill," said Wendy. "But I bet you were good, anyway."

"The only good thing about my act was that it didn't last long," I told her. "The curtain went up, and I saw all those people—it looked like about a million of them. I closed my eyes, took a deep breath, opened my mouth to sing—and threw up."

"Oh, no!" Wendy gasped.

"Oh, yes." I sighed. "All over my shoes, all over the stage, all over the chicken. I could hear Mom moaning from backstage. After that, I don't remember much—just driving back home with nobody talking. I never did get to sing my song. We didn't even bother to pick up the ribbon that everyone got just for entering."

"So that's it!" Wendy said. "That's why you won't enter beauty contests."

"That's part of it," I agreed. "But don't tell anyone. Even after all these years, it's still a little embarrassing."

Wendy shot me an indignant glare. "What kind of friend do you think I am? Of course I won't tell. But, Jill, don't you think you're making too much out of the whole thing? After all, it happened a long time ago. And if

Jessica likes those contests, what does it hurt?"

"But that's all she and Mom ever think about!" I said.

"You know," Wendy said, chewing on the end of her ponytail, "I used to feel the same way about my brother Mike and his baseball games. You've seen his baseball trophies at my house, all over the mantel. I can remember wanting to pick them all up and throw them in the fireplace."

"Yeah? You never told me that before."

"I guess I was kind of embarrassed to have been such a bratty little kid," she admitted. "It got so Mike and I couldn't be in the same room for ten seconds without yelling at each other. And the worst part was, I thought Mom and Dad didn't care about anything except him and his baseball games."

"So what did you do about it?" I asked.

"Well," she remembered, "when things got so bad I couldn't take it anymore, I finally broke down and talked to Mom. She was surprised—I don't think she and Dad knew how much they'd been bragging about Mike and ignoring me. Anyway, we had a big family conference and talked for hours.

It helped to get it all out in the open, I guess, because things got better after that. Not all at once, but they did get better. Maybe you could try the same thing. It sounds to me as if you and your mom and Jessica need to try to understand each other a little better."

I thought it over. "Well, maybe," I said at last. "I'm not sure it would help, though. Mom's just as hung up on this beauty contest thing as Jessica is."

Just then Amy and Stephanie and Rachel and a bunch of the other kids came into the room, talking and giggling and poking each other.

"Hey, Jill!" Stephanie called. "I just saw the cast list for the play. Congratulations—you'll make a great Auntie Em."

"Yeah!" Rachel echoed. "And guess who's going to be Dorothy? Paige Underwood."

"Who else?" Amy shrugged. "Anyway, I'm glad for you, Jill. I know you wanted that part."

"Thank you," I said. "I guess I'm pretty happy about it."

"What about you, Wendy?" Rachel asked.

"I'll be a Munchkin," Wendy said. "And I really want to work on the set and scenery crew. I just can't wait to paint the Emerald City—I already have some great ideas. How about you guys?"

"I'm the Good Witch," Amy said, twirling one lock of her naturally curly hair around her fingers. "My mom said if I got the part she'd make me a special dress and a crown and everything."

"You'll be perfect for that," Wendy said. "You even look like the Good Witch in the movie."

We spent the next few minutes talking about costumes and rehearsals. I could still hardly believe this was me talking about being up on stage and wearing a costume and having hundreds of people looking at me. Maybe a little bit of Jessica has rubbed off on me after all, I thought. Thank goodness Auntie Em didn't have to carry a chicken.

The day the cast was posted was one of the best days I had in all my sixth-grade year. At recess, in the lunchroom, when we went down the hall to the music room, people kept coming up to congratulate me. And they all said they thought I'd make a great Auntie Em. I started to daydream about being a movie star, with thousands of people begging me to sign their autograph books. I felt like a celebrity!

All day long I could hardly wait for that last bell to ring. I planned how I'd break the wonderful news to my mother that her daughter—her first-born child—actually had a part in the sixth-grade play. What would she say? What would she do? Maybe she'd be so excited she'd insist that we all go out for pizza and banana splits to celebrate!

I hoped she wouldn't be late getting home from the office. If she was, I thought I'd probably explode from holding the news inside.

CHAPTER FOUR

My Big Announcement

"Why do you keep looking out the window?" Jessica asked that evening. "Mom only got off work fifteen minutes ago—if she even got off on time tonight. And if the doctor had a lot of patients today she might not get home for a long time yet."

"What makes you think I'm looking for Mom?" I said, a little grumpily. "It's a free country, isn't it? A person can look out her own front window if she wants to, can't she?"

"Well, excuse *me*!" Jessica said, in a huff. "Someone around here is in a pretty bad mood."

"That just goes to show how much *you* know!" I snapped. "And for your information, Jessica Sue Armstrong, I am in a *wonderful* mood. I have never been in a better mood in all my life. In fact, *nobody* has ever been in a better mood than *I* happen to be in at this very moment."

"Oh, yeah?" She looked at me suspiciously. "What are you in such a good mood about?"

"None of your business. It's probably nothing a fourth grader could understand, anyway."

"What's that supposed to mean?" She threw down the magazine she had been reading, *1001 Great Spring Hairstyles*, and sprang to her feet. "Anything you can understand, *I* can understand. You think you're so smart! Well, I'm just as smart as you are. And besides—"

"Oh, dry up," I snapped. "Here comes Mom right now. At least give me a chance to talk to her for thirty seconds before you start in with your Atlantic City stuff, okay? I have big news for her, and I want to tell her without having to outyell *you*."

She just had time to stick her tongue out at me before we heard Mom's key in the front door, and then Mom came in, peeling her jacket off and stepping out of her shoes the minute she was in the hallway.

"Hi, girls," she said, turning to hang her jacket on the coat tree. "Oh, you picked up the mail. Good."

She grabbed a handful of bills and advertisements from the hall table and began leafing through them as she started back toward the kitchen.

"Mom!" I yelled, scrambling up from my place on the carpet beside the front window. "Mom, I need to talk to you! I've got great news!"

"Have you?" She sounded a little absentminded, and I saw that she was standing beside the kitchen sink, reading a letter she had just pulled out of a long brown envelope. As I came into the kitchen, she laid it down on the counter and smiled at me. "Well, what is it, kiddo? I'll bet you got an A on that history test you were so worried about, right?"

"No," I said. "That is—well, yes, I did, but that isn't what I wanted to tell you. This is really *important* news."

She laughed. "Well, I'm all ears," she said. "Sounds like something big. Shoot."

I tried to look modest. "I got the part," I said. "The part I tried out for in the school play. I got it!"

Her face shone as if someone had put a light bulb inside it. "Really?" she said. "You got the part? Oh, Jill, I can't believe it! My own little girl is going to play Dorothy in *The Wizard of Oz*!"

My smile seemed to be slipping a little. Why hadn't I told Mom which part I was trying out for? I should have known she'd expect me to go for the lead! "Uh—not exactly, Mom," I mumbled. "I didn't try out for Dorothy. Paige Underwood got that part."

"Oh." She looked a little confused. "What part exactly did you get, Jill? The Wicked Witch, maybe? That's a nice part, too."

I sighed. I should never have kept it a secret that I was trying out for Auntie Em. All of a sudden I hated to say it. "I—um, I'm going to be Auntie Em."

"Auntie Em?" A little pucker appeared on her forehead, as if she were trying to remember exactly who Auntie Em was. "Oh—you mean Dorothy's old aunt? The one in Kansas? I remember now. Why, that's—that's very nice, Jill. Congratulations. I'm very proud of you."

"Thanks," I said. I felt like a balloon with all the air let out. "Thanks a lot, Mom."

"Jessica," Mom said to my sister, who was standing behind me in the kitchen doorway. "Did you hear your sister's big news? She gets to be Auntie Em in the spring play! Isn't that nice?"

"Yeah," Jessica said. "Nice."

Then, when Mom's back was turned, she whispered, "Big deal! *That* was your wonderful news? Excuse me if I don't faint." And she opened the refrigerator and rummaged inside for the orange juice.

"When is your play, Jill?" Mom had opened the cabinet and was taking down a can of tuna and a box of macaroni. Tuna casserole again. So much for my daydreams of pizza and banana splits.

"I'm not sure, exactly," I said. "Sometime in April. I'm sure they'll tell us soon."

"Well, we'll be there, right in the middle of the front row," Mom said, opening a can of mushroom soup. "Right, Jessica?"

"Sure, Mom." Jessica smirked at me. There was a ring of orange juice all around her mouth, but somehow she still managed to look sickeningly adorable. "Wouldn't miss it for the world."

"You know, you had some pretty good news in the mail yourself, Jessica." Mom pointed to the brown envelope on the counter. "That's a letter from the committee of the Little Miss Apple Blossom contest—that big pageant down at Lake of the Ozarks. They accepted your entry—you're in!"

Jessica stopped drinking orange juice. "Really?" she gasped. "Wow, that really *is* great news, Mom! They don't let just anybody enter that thing, you know! I had to send them a picture, and an essay, and—"

"I know!" Mom was grinning from ear to ear now, and her face was glowing, just the way it had for a minute there when she thought I was going to be Dorothy. "This will be the biggest contest you've ever competed in. And you know what I heard? I heard that the woman who was Miss America two years ago was once a Little Miss Apple Blossom, when she was your age. So it just goes to show you; if you win this one, there's nothing you can't do!"

Jessica was jumping up and down. "Oh, Mom, I'll have to have a new formal. And I found a new way to try my hair—it's in my magazine. You take it all to the side of your face and clip it with a big gold clip, and then you make curls that go—"

"Miss Carnine said this was going to be the best play the sixth grade ever put on," I interrupted loudly.

My mother smiled at me. "And I'm sure it will be, too," she said. "It's going to be a very nice play . . . oh, and Jessica, I thought this time we might try a different talent selection. That mountain piece is cute, of course, but for a pageant this big—"

And they were off. Might as well try to talk over a hurricane, I thought gloomily, as I helped myself to a handful of cookies from the jar on the counter. Nobody even noticed that I was eating cookies before dinner. Of course, what would it matter if *I* got fat and pimply? *I* wasn't going to be in a beauty pageant. And Auntie Em was probably on the plump side, anyway.

I sighed as I plopped down on the sofa in front of the TV and turned on the cartoons. Usually I thought I was too old for cartoons, but if I turned the sound up loud enough, at least it would drown out the talk from the kitchen. If I heard the word "pageant" one more time, I'd scream.

So much for my great news. What made me think the stupid sixth-grade play was so terrific, anyway? I wondered, biting into a chocolate-chip cookie. Why did I even bother to try?

CHAPTER FIVE

Dreams

Rehearsals for *The Wizard of Oz* began the next Monday morning. Mom had to leave the house early to get me to school by seven o'clock, but she didn't complain. Actually she was pretty nice about it, even though I knew she was probably losing sleep. I couldn't figure her out. Sometimes I thought the play didn't matter to her at all—she only seemed interested in that stupid pageant Jessica was entering. But sometimes, when she went out of her way to help me—driving me to school early and offering to make my costume—sometimes I thought she really did care.

The first morning we didn't get much rehearsing done. Mostly we just milled around in the auditorium and bumped into each other and read through our lines. Miss Carnine said we shouldn't worry about it, though. "Every play starts out this way," she told us. "It takes shape gradually—like Jell-O. You'll see."

By the end of the week I began to see what she meant. Paige Underwood was going to be a great Dorothy, you could tell—of course, everyone had known that all along. And Brent Harrigan, who played the Tin Man, was pretty good, too. We had to remind Stuart Jennings, our Cowardly Lion, to speak up, and some of the Munchkins spent too much time goofing off, pushing each other, and making funny faces behind Miss Carmine's back. But the whole thing wasn't that bad. It was exciting to see all of us getting better every day, and to imagine how good we'd be by the night of the play.

On Friday morning, Miss Carnine even complimented me, right there on stage in front of the rest of the class. "Great, Jill!"

she called out. "You said that line just right!"

That felt so good, I decided I'd probably love Miss Carnine forever, even if she did make us sing too many scales.

It was then I made up my mind about something else, too. I decided I was going to be the best actor in the sixth-grade play. Oh, I wasn't going to steal the show from Paige Underwood, I knew that—after all, she had the lead part, and Auntie Em wasn't nearly as splashy. But people were going to say, "Did you see that girl who played Auntie Em? Wasn't she terrific? It was almost like watching the movie!" And then, when the play was over, my mother would probably rush backstage and put her arms around me and say, "I've never been as proud of *anyone* as I am of you!"

I loved the play. Maybe that was why Jessica seemed even harder to take than usual. I decided she must be jealous, because she saw how great I was going to be in the play. But that didn't make it any easier to put up with her and her immature stunts. Every time I tried to study my lines or do my homework, there she was, practicing her latest talent number, or eating crackers on my bed and

getting crumbs all over it, or whining because I wouldn't drop everything and play
some dumb game with her. Sure, sometimes
I lost my temper and yelled at her. Who
wouldn't? I couldn't believe that she was still
such a big baby.

"I don't know what to do with you two!"
Mom exploded one evening, when we had
argued for fifteen minutes about who got the
last hot roll. "You never were angels, I guess,
but I know you used to behave better than
this! It's as if you don't even like each other
anymore!"

"What's to like?" I smarted off, snatching
the roll out of the basket, right under
Jessica's nose.

"Mo-ooom!" she whined.

Mom lost it completely then. "All right!"
she snapped. "That's it! I'll do the dishes
myself tonight—right now I don't think I
want to see either of you ever again! You can
both march upstairs to your room, and close
the door! And you'd better not be fighting
up there, either, because if I hear one peep
out of either of you—*just one*—"

She didn't finish, but she didn't have to.
The look in her eyes was enough.

We didn't argue any more that night, but that didn't stop us from getting into it the next night, and the one after that. It wasn't like we hadn't ever fought before—Mom always used to say we had our first fight the day after she brought Jessica home from the hospital. But I guess things had never been quite *this* bad before. And the worst thing about it was that I was almost *enjoying* it.

Mom and Jessica didn't understand me at all, I thought. And I certainly didn't understand *them*. What was so wonderful about a tacky rhinestone crown and a bunch of droopy roses? My mom and sister and I might as well have come from different planets, for all we had in common.

"What are you looking at, Mom?" I asked, wandering into the den one evening, feeling bored and looking for something to do. I'd gotten all my homework done early, and I was tired of studying my lines for the play. There wasn't anything good on television, and the house was quiet because Jessica was at her best friend's house, doing the silly things fourth graders do when they get together. So when I saw Mom curled up on the couch with a thick scrapbook, I pounced. Even spending the evening looking at old pictures would be better than nothing.

Mom jumped when I plopped down beside her, as if she had been a million miles away. "Huh? Oh, hi, Jill. I'm just looking at my scrapbook, from the days when I was in beauty pageants."

"Oh, yeah." I looked at the old photographs and yellowed pages of the book on her lap. "I don't think I ever saw this scrapbook before," I said. "How come?"

Mom shrugged and turned a page. "I guess I never thought you'd be interested," she said. "I know beauty pageants aren't exactly your favorite thing."

I craned my neck to get a better look. "Is that *you*, Mom?" I gasped, staring at a big picture of a beautiful girl in a long white formal, with her arms full of roses and a glittery crown on her head. "You were gorgeous!"

"Thanks." She smiled. "Yep, that was your old mom, all right. This was taken on the night I won the Queen of the May pageant. I think I was seventeen. Can you believe that hairdo? And that awful lipstick!"

"Yeah, but you looked really good," I insisted. "Did you win any other contests?"

She looked at me. "I'm sure I've told you about all this before," she said.

I shrugged, feeling a little sheepish. "I—I guess I don't always listen," I admitted. "It's like you said, beauty pageants aren't my thing."

She turned a few more pages in her scrapbook. "Here," she said, pointing to another picture. "This was the night I was crowned Peach Princess. And this one—oh, this was a big one, Queen of the Autumnfest. But my biggest one—well, here, I'll show you."

She flipped through the book until she came to a picture of a group of glamorous young women on a stage. "Look here, Jill. This was a night I'll never forget."

"You were beautiful!" I breathed. "But you didn't win this one, Mom. Another girl is wearing the crown. And your sash says 'First Runner-Up.' "

"Look what the *winner's* sash says." Mom pointed.

I squinted at the photo, and then stared up into my mother's face.

"But this"—I gasped—"this says *Miss Missouri*! You mean you were—"

Mom nodded. "First runner-up in the Miss Missouri pageant," she said. "I came *that close* to going to Atlantic City for the Miss America pageant." Her eyes got that familiar dreamy look. "Sometimes I still think about it," she said. "Every September, when the pageant is on TV, I imagine that's me up there, with the flashbulbs flashing, and the music playing, and everyone applauding . . ." She laughed. "I guess you think your mom is pretty silly, huh?"

"Well, Mom," I protested, "even if I'm not wild about beauty contests, I have to admit that Miss America is a pretty big deal. But I don't understand—if it meant that much to you, why did you stop entering pageants? Why didn't you keep on until you got to Atlantic City? You were pretty enough."

She shook her head as she gently closed the scrapbook and laid it carefully on the coffee table, as if it were made of the most delicate crystal. "Things got in the way, I guess," she said. "Right after the pageant, I met your dad, and it wasn't long before the two of us were married and having you kids.

I didn't even think about pageants then; I was too busy learning how to change diapers and make meat loaf and hold down a job at the same time. There was no time for things like crowns and roses."

I felt something inside me twist. "Does that mean"—I swallowed—"does that mean that you're sorry you married Dad and had Jessica and me? Your life would have been more exciting as Miss America."

She looked surprised. "Maybe so, but I wouldn't trade you girls and my memories of your dad for all the rhinestones in Atlantic City. No, I guess my dreams just changed, that's all, and that happens to everyone when they grow up." She sighed. "Well, that's enough of that." She picked up the scrapbook and put it back in the bookshelf. "Hey, I'll tell you what, let's run down to the video store and see if we can't find a good movie to rent. Then we can make popcorn and curl up for a nice quiet evening together, just the two of us."

"Hey, great!" As I ran for my jacket, I thought about the look on Mom's face while she stared at that old scrapbook.

My own mom, first runner-up to Miss

Missouri, and I hadn't even known about it! I couldn't help feeling a little mad at myself. Maybe I should have paid more attention. Maybe I should have listened to Mom's stories instead of tuning her and Jessica out the way I usually did.

That evening, as Mom and I shared a big bowl of popcorn and laughed at the movie, I caught myself staring at her a lot, as if I were seeing her for the first time. She looked different to me—I wasn't just seeing good ol' Mom anymore. I was seeing that pretty girl in the long white dress, her arms full of flowers and her eyes full of dreams.

And suddenly I understood, just a little, why Jessica's pageants were so important to Mom. Not that Jessica wasn't still a stuck-up little snot. But I could imagine the way Mom must have felt all those years ago, and how Jessica reminded her of when she was young.

After three weeks of before-school rehearsals, Miss Carnine gave all of us with lead parts permission slips for Saturday rehearsals at school. "Make sure your parents sign the forms, and be here at two," she announced. "You should expect rehearsals to last till four-thirty or five. And those of you who already have your costumes done should bring them, too, so I can look them over. Hey, John Paul—and the Munchkin in the back row—the next time I see you two shoving anyone, you'll both go to the principal's office! Is that understood?"

"Do you have your costume done yet?" Wendy asked me at lunch that day.

I took a swallow of milk. "Not yet," I said. "Mom's going to make it, but so far she hasn't had time. She's been sewing late every night, trying to get a costume finished for some contest Jessica's going to be in Saturday afternoon. But as soon as she gets that done, I guess she'll get around to mine. Hey, I just thought—if Mom's going to be at that contest with Jessica, how am I going to get to practice Saturday? I guess I'll have to hitch a ride with Amy or Rachel or one of the others, since you don't have to come."

"Hey," Wendy asked, "what contest is Jessica in this week? Anything big?"

I shrugged. "To the little princess, they're *all* big," I said. "This one is Adorable Miss, or something pukey like that. Who knows, and who cares?"

Wendy looked over her sandwich at me. "That's mean," she said.

"Maybe so, Wendy, but you should just try living with her. If her head gets any bigger, Mom's going to have to build on a room just for her—with an extra-wide door."

Wendy sighed. "Well," she said, "I think it's too bad you can't get along. I've always *wanted* a sister, you know."

"Count your blessings." I sneered. "Or better yet, help yourself to Jessica. I'd never miss her."

I expected Wendy to laugh, but instead she got very quiet as she finished her bologna-and-cheese sandwich. I stared at her, and the last bite of my peanut-butter sandwich felt like wet cement in my mouth.

"Wendy, what's gotten into you?" I said, when I had finally forced the gooey lump down my throat. "I thought you were my friend."

"I am!" she said, folding her napkin as she

spoke. "But I hardly know you anymore. You're so busy being jealous of Jessica, you don't think about anything else. Everything you do is just so you can be better than Jessica, or get more attention than Jessica, or show Jessica up. Is it so terrible just being *Jill*?"

CHAPTER SIX

Hands Off My Pookie!

After all our terrific practices before school, our first Saturday rehearsal didn't go so great. Everyone forgot lines, dropped things, stood in the wrong place. Even Amy's fuzzy little dog, Peaches, who was playing the part of Toto, drove us all crazy running around, yipping, and nipping at the Cowardly Lion's heels. "What's gotten into you kids, anyway?" Miss Carnine snapped, as we gathered around her after rehearsal. "Do you want to be the first sixth grade not to do a play? Because that's exactly what is going to happen if you don't get on the ball—I could call the whole thing off!"

"Not so great, huh?" Rachel muttered, as we headed for her mother's car.

"Not so great," I agreed. I kicked a pebble on the sidewalk, sending it rattling into the bushes. My head hurt, and my shoulders were cramped from sitting around so long. I hoped the evening would go better than the afternoon. I was in such a bad mood, all I needed was for someone to look at me cross-eyed and I'd make them wish they hadn't.

Mom's car was in the driveway when I got home, but there was no sign of her or Jessica as I let myself into the house and ran up the stairs to my bedroom. I'd flop down on the bed for a few minutes and read a magazine or something, I thought. Then, when I wasn't so tired, I'd have a few chocolate-chip cookies to take my mind off my terrible afternoon.

I threw my bedroom door open, and—

There lay Jessica in the middle of *my* bed, with her shoes on *my* bedspread and *my* pillow all scrunched up under her head. That was bad enough, but what was even worse, she had *my* Pookie squeezed in her arms, hugging him as if he were hers!

Pookie is my teddy bear. Twelve may be a little old for teddy bears, but Pookie was always special. I'd had him since I was just a little kid—in fact, Pookie was the last birthday present my dad ever gave me, just a few weeks before he died. Maybe that was the reason that old teddy bear meant so much to me. Sometimes, when I was sad, I'd hug him close and cry until his fur was wet. And nobody—*nobody*—was ever supposed to touch him, or talk to him, or even *look* at him, but me.

For a second or two, I was too angry to say anything, or even to move. I just stood there in the doorway with my mouth hanging open, feeling my face start to burn. Then I heard myself squawk, and the next thing I knew I was standing by my bed, yanking Pookie away from Jessica so hard I heard a few of his stitches pop.

"What are you doing with my *Pookie*?" I wailed, looking him over for damage. "And what are you doing on my bed? Get off, you little creep, or—"

She pushed herself up on one elbow and wiped one hand across her face. For the first time, I noticed that her eyes looked red and swollen. Now what was wrong with *her*? I wondered.

"I didn't know you were home already," she said. "I wasn't hurting your bear, Jill, honest. I just—"

"Of course you were hurting him!" I snarled. "You were *touching* him, weren't you? Now get off my bed!"

"Please, Jill!" She made a little hiccupping sound that sounded almost like a sob. "I've been waiting for you for a long time. I need to talk to you, and I thought you wouldn't mind if—"

Just then I saw the rip in Pookie's back seam, where I had tugged him away from Jessica. The stuffing was poking right out!

"Look what you've done!" I shrieked, shoving Pookie toward her. "Look what you've done to my Pookie, you little mo-ron!"

Now she really did begin to cry, the tears spilling quickly down her cheeks. "I didn't mean to, Jill!" she sobbed.

I didn't even know I was going to hit Jessica until I felt my hand sting where it had slapped her, hard, right across the cheek. The sound the slap made echoed like a gun-shot, and for a second or two I was so sur-prised I just stood there, staring at my hand, and then at Jessica's face, where the print of my fingers made bright red stripes. "Oh, Jess," I began, feeling as if my stomach dropped. "I don't—I didn't mean . . ."

"You jerk!" she roared, jumping up from the bed. The next thing I knew, her hands were tangled in my hair, yanking till I felt tears in my eyes. And then there we were, like a couple of spitting cats—shoving and hitting and rolling around on my bed, mak-ing so much noise we didn't even hear Mom running down the hall.

"Girls!" The sound of her angry voice made us jump apart as if someone had emp-tied a bucket of ice water over our heads. "Girls, what on earth—? Stop that this in-stant, do you hear me?"

We looked at each other, and then at her. We were both breathing hard. Jessica's face was still red where I had slapped her, and my scalp felt as if it was on fire where she had yanked at my hair. Neither one of us said a word—we just stood there, glaring at each other.

"Well?" Mom demanded. "What is going on here?"

When neither one of us answered, she walked across the room with a deep sigh, took Jessica by the shoulders, and turned her toward the bedroom door. "March," she said. "Downstairs—wait for me in the den. I want to talk to Jill first, but you'll have your turn."

When Jessica had gone, sobbing all the way down the stairs, Mom turned and looked at me for a long moment without saying a word. Her eyes looked tired.

"Well, Jill," she asked quietly, "what was it? Why were you and your sister trying to tear each other to pieces?"

I could feel my bottom lip sticking out. "She had my *Pookie*," I tried to explain. "She *ripped* him—right here, see?"

Mom rubbed her forehead. "That was it?" she asked. "A *teddy bear*? *That's* what caused all this uproar?"

Her tone of voice made me feel pretty stupid. But I wasn't going to give up.

"But he's the very last present Dad ever gave me, remember? And Jessica was on *my* bed, and she was using *my* pillow. And I'm tired of the way she always—"

"Honestly, Jill!" My mother's face tightened into a scowl. "I might have expected this kind of thing from you a few years ago, but I thought you were more grown up now. After all, aren't you the one who's always reminding me that you're in the sixth grade? First grade's more like it, with the behavior I just saw!"

"But what about her?" That whine was back in my voice, and I hated myself for it, but I couldn't stop. "Why don't you ever get mad at *her*? She can do anything she wants, and she never gets in trouble! Why aren't you yelling at *Jessica*?"

I could tell by the way Mom clenched her fists that she was trying not to lose her temper. "In case you weren't paying attention," she said quickly, in a low voice, "I just told your sister that I would be downstairs to talk to her in a few minutes. Also, you might like to know, it happens that Jessica does have a reason to be upset this evening."

"Oh, yeah?" I snorted. "What's that? Did she break a fingernail? Or maybe she ran out of lipstick?"

Mom looked sad as she shook her head. "Jessica had a pageant this afternoon, remember?" she said. "A fairly big one, and she had her heart set on winning. Well, she didn't—she was first runner-up, but she didn't win. And yes, I know what you're going to say—So what? And I also know that winning isn't everything. But you have to remember that Jessica is only nine, and she doesn't know how to handle disappointment very well yet. She'd been waiting in this room for over an hour for you to get home—I can't imagine why, but for some reason she thought it would make her feel better to talk things over with her big sister. Maybe *that's* why she was cuddling your teddy bear. Maybe she needed a friend, even if it was just a stuffed animal."

Sometimes Mom has a way of making me feel about three inches tall.

"I—I didn't know that," I mumbled, looking down at Pookie, who was now dangling limply from my hand. "She should have said something."

Mom looked straight into my eyes. "Did you give her a chance?"

"But she should have known Pookie is off-limits. He's *mine*," I tried again, feeling less sure of myself every second.

"Yes," Mom agreed. "Yes, he's yours, and I understand why you're so attached to him. But Jessica's your sister. Sometimes I wonder if that matters to you. I'm going downstairs now and have a little talk with her. I'll call you when dinner is ready."

As I watched her go, I remembered what Wendy had said in the lunchroom. *You're so busy being jealous of Jessica, you don't think about anything else.* I really wasn't myself anymore. I felt mean. And empty, like my teddy bear with all his stuffing leaking out. And I knew what I needed to do.

"Mom?" I called, just as she had started down the stairs. "Mom, when you're finished talking to Jessica, could—could you ask her to come up here? I—I think maybe the two of us have a few things to talk over, too."

Mom stared at me. "All right," she said. "I'll tell her, but it's up to her whether she wants to come or not."

Ten long minutes later, the bedroom door

edged open, an inch at a time, and Jessica's tearstained face peeked in carefully, as if she thought I might be planning to throw something at her.

"Oh, come on in, Jessica." I sighed, wearily sitting down on the edge of my bed. "I'm not going to hurt you."

She slouched into the room, her hands buried in her jeans pockets, her shoulders slumped.

"I didn't mean to hurt your bear," she mumbled, scuffing at the carpet with one tennis shoe.

I fidgeted with the lace trim of my bedspread so I wouldn't have to look her in the eye.

"I know," I said. "And I'm really sorry I hit you. I guess I went crazy for a minute. I don't know why I did that."

"It's okay," she said. "I know you're weird about Pookie because Dad gave him to you. I usually never touch him. I just had this really rotten day—" she began, but she choked on her words.

"Funny," I said. "I was about to tell you the same thing." Jessica sat down on her bed.

"We fight all the time, don't we? It didn't used to be like this, did it?"

"I don't remember." I looked at her and saw that she was blinking back tears. "You seem to be mad at me all the time. Do you hate me, Jill?"

I gasped. "No! I—I guess I act like it sometimes, but I don't hate you. You're my sister. You can't hate your own *sister*. I'm sorry, Jess; honest I am."

She ducked her head and managed to grin at me. Even with grimy tear streaks all over her face, I had to admit that she still looked adorable.

"I sort of understand," she whispered. "I'm sorry, too. Let's not ever fight like that again. Okay, Jill?"

"Never again," I promised solemnly. "Oh, and Jess—Mom told me about your pageant today. Do you think some milk and cookies would make you feel better?"

"I think so," she said.

"Chocolate chip or peanut butter?" I asked.

"Peanut butter," she said, without even stopping to think about it.

"You got it."

As I hurried to the kitchen, I felt better than I had in weeks. Who knows, I thought, maybe this sisterhood stuff wouldn't turn out to be so bad after all.

CHAPTER SEVEN

A Star—Me?

"Jill Armstrong?" The principal's secretary stood in the doorway of the sixth-grade classroom, calling my name, and I felt my heart start to pound. What had I done wrong now? "I have a message from Miss Carnine for Jill Armstrong."

Mrs. Shanahan took the folded note and held it out to me. "Better see what she wants, Jill," she said.

I hated to open the note, remembering the way I had goofed up my lines in rehearsal last Saturday. What if Miss Carnine was writing to say that she was replacing me with someone else, someone who'd make a better Auntie Em? And Mom had started working on my costume just last night!

Everyone in the room was staring at me as I unfolded the paper and read the note, written in Miss Carnine's big, fancy handwriting.

"Dear Jill," the note said. "I need to talk to you about something important. Will you drop by the music room before you leave the building tonight?"

And I knew I had been right. Miss Carnine was going to drop me from the play. I wasn't good enough even to be Auntie Em.

I missed three spelling words and completely flunked a math quiz that afternoon. My whole body ached, with that numbness you get the minute you step into a doctor's office for a shot. Why couldn't I do anything right? Why couldn't I even manage a part like Auntie Em?

And what would Mom and Jessica say when I told them? Poor Mom; she'd be just as disappointed as I was. Jessica, too—in fact, while we were having our talk on Sat-

urday, she had even said that she was looking forward to seeing me in the play. That
had made me feel really good. Now that I
thought of it, we had hardly fought at all
since that talk. We were even starting to act
like sisters again, part of the time. Now—
well, I didn't look forward to telling Jessica
that she didn't have any reason to be proud
of me after all.

Sometimes I thought I couldn't wait for
the last bell to ring, and sometimes I hoped
it never would. It was a long, long afternoon. When 3:15 finally came, Wendy
walked down to the music room with me.
"I'll wait right out here," she whispered.
"And don't look so scared—it's probably not
anything bad at all."

"Sure," I said. "That's probably what they
told Marie Antoinette, right before they
chopped her head off." And I took a deep
breath, opened the music room door, and
marched in.

Miss Carnine was grading tests at her
desk, but she looked up when she saw me.

"Oh, Jill!" she said, smiling and pushing
her glasses back to the top of her head.

"Thanks for coming so quickly, dear. There's something I need to discuss with you."

"I—I think I know what it is," I croaked, through a mouth that felt as dry as cotton.

"You do?" She looked surprised. "Now, how could you have heard about it already? *I* just decided this morning."

I wasn't too proud to beg. "Please, Miss Carnine," I pleaded, "don't do it! I'll try harder, I promise. You'll see—I can do it, I know I can. Don't take my part away from me!"

Her mouth dropped open, and she stared at me for a second or two. "Is *that* what you thought?" she said at last. "You really thought I called you down here to tell you you weren't going to be Auntie Em?"

I nodded. "Isn't it?" I asked.

Now she laughed. "Well, in a way, yes," she said. "I guess it is."

I felt the tears gathering behind my eyelids. "Oh, please, Miss Carnine—" I began.

She held up one hand. "For goodness sake, calm down, Jill! You didn't even give me a chance to finish. Yes, I called you down to tell you that I'm giving the part of Auntie

Em to Rhonda Tillman—but only because there's another part I want you to play."

"Another part?" I asked suspiciously. "A—a Munchkin?"

"Not a Munchkin!" She was laughing again. "No, Jill, I want you to be—" She stopped, and I almost heard a drumroll. "I want you to be Dorothy!"

I gasped, stepped back, stumbled over a wastebasket, and just barely managed to land in a chair. "Don't tease about things like that, Miss Carnine," I begged. "It's not funny."

She shook her head. "I'm not trying to be funny," she said. "I really do want you to be Dorothy."

"But—but—" I was getting more confused by the second. "But what about Paige Underwood? She's a terrific Dorothy!"

"Yes, she is," Miss Carnine agreed. "But her father found out yesterday that he's being transferred to his company's plant in Dallas. They're going to move next week. So Paige won't be here to play Dorothy. And I want you to take her place."

My head was whirling. "But I can't do that!" I said. "Please, I can't play Dorothy,

Miss Carnine. Not after Paige! She can sing, she can dance, she can act. And I—"

"And you can do all those things, too," she insisted firmly. "Just as well as Paige, although I know you don't believe that." She leaned forward across her desk and spoke in a very low voice. "Can I tell you a secret, Jill? I was hoping that you would try out for that part in the first place. I thought you'd make a great Dorothy. But you didn't, and I had to settle for giving you the Auntie Em part. But now—well, I don't think anyone else could learn such a big part so fast, or do so good a job as you. So I'd like you to give it a try."

I was dizzy. Everything was happening so fast.

"I don't know," I said. "I just—"

"The sixth grade needs you," Miss Carnine coaxed. "*I* need you. You'll be fine; wait and see. You may need some extra coaching to learn the part by the end of the month, but I'll help with that. Mrs. Shanahan says she'll even give you time out from class to work with me. What do you say? Do we have a new star?"

I think the word "star" made up my mind.

I recalled the look on my mother's face for those few seconds when she thought I was actually going to be Dorothy. Now I imagined the way she'd look when I came home and told her it was true after all.

And Jessica would have to share the spotlight with me.

"I'll do it," I said, and Miss Carnine gave me a big, relieved smile. "I don't know *how* I'll do it, but I'll play Dorothy. I've got to tell you, though; just thinking about it makes me shake."

She smiled. "I think I can understand that," she said. "I am asking a lot of you. But I wouldn't ask if I didn't think you could do it."

I gulped. "You won't be sorry, Miss Carnine," I promised. "I'm not sure how, but I'm going to be a great Dorothy. In fact, I'm going to be the best Dorothy ever—and that's a promise!"

"Oh, Jill, honey, that's just *wonderful*!" My mother hugged me as tight as I always hugged Pookie. "My very own daughter, star of the sixth-grade play! Jessica, isn't that terrific news?"

Jessica didn't exactly jump up and down, but she did smile at me. "I'm really happy for you, Jill," she said. "I bet you'll be a great Dorothy."

"Gosh, thanks, Jessica," I answered.

As my sister went back to painting her fingernails bubble-gum pink, I stared at her. She actually sounded *happy* for me. Maybe things really were changing.

"Oh, we have so much to *do*!" My attention snapped back to Mom, who was listing things and counting them off on her fingers. "There's a new costume to make—I wonder if Rhonda can use the Auntie Em costume I started?—and we'll want to buy lots and lots of film, and I can help you with your lines . . ."

As we made plans, it finally began to seem real to me. I was actually going to be Dorothy in the sixth-grade play! And for the first time ever, I thought I understood how Mom and Jessica felt when they were getting ready for a big pageant. It was great to feel important. In fact, it was the greatest feeling in the world!

CHAPTER EIGHT

I Should Have Known

During the first week in April, we began putting the whole play together—lines, songs, and dances. Of course, everyone else was more prepared than I was; Dorothy had so many lines and so many songs, sometimes I worried that I'd never learn them all in time. But Miss Carnine spent hours coaching me before and after school, and I started to think that maybe—just maybe—I'd do okay after all.

"Of course you will," my mother said, when I told her about it. "You're a natural-born star. I always knew you could be!"

Oh, yeah, I couldn't help thinking. Then how come you never said so before?

But mostly I was just happy to see my mother so excited about the play. Even Jessica tossed me a compliment once in a while—mostly stuff like "Not too bad, Jill" or "You didn't goof that as much as usual this time." But it was a nice change. She even spent one whole evening fussing with my hair until it looked exactly like Dorothy's in the movie. And I overheard her talking with one of her bratty little friends on the phone, actually bragging about the fact that her sister was the star of the sixth-grade play! If I hadn't known better, I would have sworn that aliens had stolen the real Jessica and replaced her with some pod person.

But what surprised me most was the change in me. Not only was I getting along with my sister, I was beginning to enjoy being Dorothy. Every day it got a little easier for me to walk onto that stage, and my lines were coming along, too. Slowly, Miss Carnine ironed the wrinkles out of the play. The Cowardly Lion learned to dance without tripping over his tail. The Wicked Witch developed a spooky cackle. And the Munchkins finally stopped goofing off and got their act together. I started to feel sure that Dorothy would, too.

"Class, our posters arrived from the printer today," Miss Carnine said one morning. She held a big stack of bright yellow papers. "We'll hang them all over the school, of course. But we can also take them around the neighborhood and put them up in store windows, on bulletin boards and telephone poles, and wherever else you can think of. Who wants to take some and get started?"

Almost all of us waved our hands, and Miss Carnine carefully divided the stack of posters so each of us got six or seven.

"Put them anyplace where a lot of people will see them," she instructed. "Let's try for a full house on the night of the play. And let me remind you again to be sure to mark your calendars for Friday, April 30. Don't plan anything—and I do mean *anything*—else for that night."

I looked down at the stack of posters in my lap. I'd take one to the grocery store for sure, I planned. The manager there was nice—he'd let me tape it in the front window. The public library might let me tack one on their bulletin board, and then there was the church, and the dry cleaner, and the car wash, and . . .

I'd put up posters all over town, I decided. After all, since I was going to try to be the best Dorothy ever, I might as well have an audience!

"Mom!" I met my mother at the front door the minute she got home that night. "I've got to go around the neighborhood and put up posters for the play. Can I go right now?"

"*May* I," Mom corrected for about the zillionth time; you'd think she would have given up after all these years. "Posters, huh? Hey, these look pretty nice. Let me see one."

Proudly, I handed her one of the bright yellow posters. "I thought I'd put one up in the grocery store," I told her. "And the library, and the pet shop, and—what's the matter, Mom?

A very strange expression clouded Mom's face as she read the poster. Her skin had gone a greenish-white color, and her shoulders suddenly slumped as she sank down into her chair.

"Oh, no," she said softly. "Oh, no. I don't believe this."

"Mom?" I was starting to feel shaky myself. "Mom, what is it? You're scaring me!"

She looked up at me, and I saw that there were tears in her eyes.

"Honey," she said, "I don't know how to tell you this."

"Tell me *what*?" I demanded impatiently. "Don't keep me in suspense—tell me *what*?"

Mom groaned. "It's Jessica's pageant," she explained. "You remember—the Little Miss Apple Blossom pageant that she wants to be in so much."

"Yeah, I remember," I said. "What about it?"

"It's the same night!" Mom said. I felt my stomach dive to the bottom of my sneakers. "Of all the rotten luck!"

"But that doesn't make any difference, does it, Mom?" I asked anxiously. "I mean, Jessica's already been in a million pageants, right? You'll still come to my play, won't you? Jessica can drop out of this one pageant, can't she, Mom? Mom?!"

The tears spilled out of my mother's eyes and began making little tracks down her cheeks.

"Oh, Jill, honey," she said. "I wish it were that easy, I really do. But we can't afford for Jessica to drop out—they won't refund the entry fee, and I've spent a fortune on her new costume and formal, too. I've invested too much in this for Jessica to drop out. Oh, and I really do want to see your play!"

I couldn't believe what I was hearing. "*What?*" I yelled. "What are you talking about, Mom? You can't mean you're not coming to my play!"

She lifted both hands toward me, then dropped them into her lap. "I don't know what to do! I just don't know!"

At that moment Jessica appeared in the doorway, a little frown puckering her forehead. "I heard yelling," she said. "What's up?"

"Oh, Jessica, it's terrible!" Mom groaned, before I had a chance to say anything. "Jill's play is the same night as the Little Miss Apple Blossom pageant! How in the world can I be both places at the same time?"

Jessica's mouth dropped open. "You're kidding!" she said. "Wow, Jill, that's really tough luck."

"Why does it have to be tough luck for *me*?" I argued desperately. "Why am I always the one who has to give in? Can't you give up just one little pageant, Jessica?"

"But it's *not* a little pageant!" Jessica looked as if she were about to cry. "It's the most important contest I've ever entered, and I can't go if Mom isn't there."

"Be quiet, girls, and let me think." Mom pressed her fingers to her forehead. "There has to be a way I can—wait!" She looked at Jessica. "Jessica, isn't your friend Danielle entering that pageant, too?"

Jessica nodded. "Yeah," she said. "So?"

"Well," Mom thought out loud, "maybe if Danielle's mother would agree to take you with them and help you a little with your hair and costume—"

"Oh, no!" Jessica wailed. "I need you there, Mom! This is important to me!"

"The play is important to your sister, too," Mom reminded her, waving one hand at me in a "let me handle this" gesture. "I've gone to all your other pageants, Jessica. It seems to me that this time it is Jill's turn. Don't you think so?"

"But—" Jessica fussed. Then she looked from Mom to me, sighed a deep sigh, and let her shoulders slump. "Oh, okay," she said. "If that's the way it has to be. I don't like it, but I guess it's fair."

"That's my girl." Mom grinned, and I hurried across the room to give Jessica a little hug.

"I'll make it up to you, Jess," I told her. "I promise I will. This means so much to me."

"Let me call Danielle's mother," Mom said. "Keep your fingers crossed, girls."

I sat there in the den, on the very edge of the couch, while Mom talked on the kitchen phone. It seemed like an hour, but finally she came back into the den. She looked tired, but there was a smile on her face.

"Well?" Jessica and I demanded in the same breath.

"Will Danielle's mom take Jessica?" I asked. "Can you come to my play?"

Mom nodded. "It's all set," she said. "I'm sorry to miss the pageant, but I'm glad I can be there for your big night, Jill. Oh, I do wish I could be in two places at once!"

I looked from Mom's exhausted face to Jessica's disappointed one.

"I have a great idea," I said. "I'll fix dinner tonight. Just to show how much I appreciate what you two are doing for me."

Mom smiled gratefully, but Jessica didn't look so sure.

"*You'll* fix dinner?" she asked. "What do you know how to cook?"

I thought for a minute. "How about soup and grilled-cheese sandwiches? And I know we have a lot of cookies left in the cookie jar for dessert."

"That sounds terrific," Mom said. "I have to admit, I'm just about done in. Thanks, Jill."

I left her and Jessica watching TV in the den while I went to rummage through the kitchen cabinets and the refrigerator for cans of vegetable soup, a jar of olives, and the makings for the sandwiches. Spreading all the stuff out on the counter, I got down to work opening cans and greasing the big skillet.

"Want some help?" Jessica asked, drifting into the kitchen a few minutes later with a big book balanced on her head, practicing her posture.

"You could set the table," I said, dumping the olives into a bowl.

To my surprise, she actually went to the cabinet and took out a pile of plates. Popping an olive into her mouth, she began setting the plates on our blue place mats. As I scooped the soup from the cans into the saucepan, I suddenly had an inspiration. As soon as the soup was ready to heat, I went out to the backyard and picked a handful of yellow daffodils, put them in Mom's favorite white vase, and set them in the middle of the table.

"What are you doing all this for?" Jessica asked, folding blue paper napkins and putting them in the middle of each plate. "Are you feeling guilty?"

I sighed. Maybe I was feeling guilty. I wasn't used to Mom choosing me over Jessica. But I said, "Can't I do something nice just because I feel like it?"

I went to the kitchen door and called to Mom that supper was ready. I made her sit down at the table, while I dished everything up and poured juice for everyone. Then I sat down across the table from Jessica. I even smiled at her as I passed her the olives and the plate full of sandwiches.

"Great dinner, Jill," Mom said, when she'd finished her cookies and ice cream.

"Oh, it wasn't much," I said, but I felt a glow inside. For once, instead of fighting, we'd all worked our problems out together. And I had to admit that was a pretty good feeling. Maybe there was hope for our family yet!

CHAPTER NINE

Life Isn't Fair

"Is that the phone?" Mom called a few nights later, running out of the bathroom with a towel wrapped around her wet hair. "Girls, please turn that TV down—I can't hear myself think! Yep, that's the phone, all right."

She made a dive for the telephone, pausing just long enough to say, "Get started on your homework, girls. Afterward, we can *all* watch TV." She picked up the phone. "Hello? Oh, hi, Evelyn. Are you and Danielle about ready for the big pageant? You don't know how much I appreciate your taking

Jessica with you. I couldn't have managed without—*What?*"

Mom's voice sounded so funny on that last word that Jessica and I exchanged worried looks. Mom was frowning and clicking her fingernails in a quick, nervous movement on the top of the phone table.

"Are you sure? I see. Oh, that's too bad. No, no, of course not. I understand, and the girls will, too. No, there's no reason to feel bad. You can't help it. Thanks anyway. I'll see you at the PTO meeting, okay? Yes, next month. Thanks for calling. Bye."

After Mom hung up the phone, she just sat there for a long moment, not saying a word. The look on her face made me uneasy.

"Mom?" I croaked. "Mom, what is it? Is something wrong?"

"Oh, girls." She sighed. "Things aren't working out at all the way we had planned."

"Things?" Jessica echoed. "What things?"

"For Jill's play and your pageant," Mom explained. "We had it all set up for you to go to the pageant with Danielle's mother, so I could see Jill's play. Now it seems that Danielle's grandmother is sick, and Danielle's mom has to fly to Cleveland tomorrow to be with her. She'll be gone for at least two weeks, and she won't be back in time for the pageant. So Danielle is going to have to drop out, which means"—she rubbed the back of her neck—"which means that you won't be able to go with them. And that leaves us back at square one: I can't be two places at once."

"Mom," I said, while Jessica looked at the floor, "this play is important to me. If you can't come, I'm not sure if I even want to be in it."

"Oh, Jill." Mom got up from her chair and gently brushed a stray wisp of hair away from my face. "You're in this play because *you* want to be in it—and you can do a great job just because you're *you*, whether I'm in the audience or not."

"And, Jill, Mom really has to go to the pageant with me," Jessica pointed out. "I couldn't go alone, even if I had a way to get there. I wish we could be at your play, too. But—"

"Oh, stop it, Jessica!" It was hard to believe I had been getting along with my little sister just a few minutes before. Now that friendly feeling was melting like snow in the sunshine. "It's not as if you haven't already won practically every contest in this whole part of the country!"

"We've been through all of that, too." Now Mom was starting to lose her patience. "I've done everything I could to get to your play, Jill, and you know it. But this is a very important pageant, and I can't afford to lose all the effort planning for it, not to mention the entry fee, which I've already paid."

"I'm sorry, Jill," Jessica said. She laid one hand on my arm, but I shook it impatiently away. "Next time Mom will go to your play."

"But there might not *be* a next time!" I insisted. "There's only one sixth-grade play—I may never be in another one. I've had to understand my whole life. If Mom can't be at my play, I don't want to be there myself!" Suddenly, scalding hot tears flooded my eyes, and I choked on a lump in my throat that seemed as big as a beachball. "Oh," I sobbed, "what's the use? What's the use of even trying?" Whirling, I ran from the den, down the hall, and up the stairs.

"Jill!" Mom called after me. I could hear her right behind me, but I was too upset to wait for her.

I threw open the bedroom door and flung myself facedown across my bed, then grabbed Pookie in a stranglehold and proceeded to soak his brown-and-gold fur with my tears.

"Oh, Jill." I didn't look up when I heard Mom's soft voice from the doorway, but a moment later I felt her hand on my back, rubbing gently between my shoulder blades. "Honey, I know it's not fair. But sometimes you just have to pick yourself up and go on. You may not believe it now, but I know exactly how you feel."

Angrily, I rolled onto my back and glared at her.

"Yeah?" I asked. "How would you know that?"

Her eyes got that strange, faraway look I had seen in them once before, the night that she and I had looked at her scrapbook together.

"Because I felt the very same way when we lost your dad," she said. "You were so young when he died—you probably don't remember him too well, do you?"

"Just a little," I admitted. "Kind of like pictures in my mind."

"He was a special person," my mother said. "Oh, Jill, I loved him so much. And he—well, he was crazy about all three of us. He called us his three best girls. I always thought we'd have years and years together, to watch you girls grow up, go to college, maybe get married and have families of your own. We had so many hopes, so many dreams. . . ." She shook her head. For a moment she seemed to have lost her voice. Then she cleared her throat and went on. "When the doctors told us he had cancer, I couldn't believe it. He was only twenty-seven years old. And as I watched him getting sicker and sicker, I learned that things don't always work out the way you plan. That's when I really found out that life isn't always fair."

Now the two of us were crying together. Looking across the room, I saw that Jessica was standing by the door, and that there were tears on her face, too.

My head was spinning. The more I tried to stop crying, the harder the tears fell. I couldn't quit shaking, and I thought I'd choke on the sobs in my throat.

Jessica's voice sounded little and solemn. "What we need is frozen yogurt," she said.

Mom and I stared at her, then at each other. Suddenly we were all laughing, just as hard as we had been crying a second before. Only laughing felt a whole lot better.

"Frozen yogurt sounds like a great idea," Mom agreed. "Last one to the car has to pay!"

"No fair!" Jessica and I squealed, scrambling for our jackets.

Mom let us beat her to the car. But then, we had known she would.

CHAPTER TEN

Butterflies on the Yellow Brick Road

I couldn't help it, though; somehow the whole idea of the play wasn't nearly as much fun after that. Just knowing Mom wasn't going to be there took the excitement out of things for me. If it hadn't been so close to the night of the play, I would have asked Miss Carnine to find someone else to play Dorothy. I was so upset, I couldn't even concentrate on learning my lines—and I still had a lot of them to learn.

"It's no use, Wendy!" I slammed my script closed and let it fall into my lap. Wendy and

I were in my bedroom, working on the hardest scene in the play, and I was about ready to give up. "I'll never learn all these lines in time! I can't do it—I can't keep my mind on things. The whole play's going to be ruined, and it's all because I can't learn these stupid lines."

Wendy—good old faithful Wendy—just wouldn't give up. We'd been through this scene at least a dozen times, but Wendy kept plugging on.

"Of course you can!" she insisted. "It wasn't so bad that last time. You almost had it, except for those lines down at the bottom of the page, see, where Dorothy's asking the Wizard if he can send her home to Kansas."

"Which only happens to be just about the most important scene in the whole play," I groaned. "If I goof up *that* scene, *nothing* is going to go right. I wish I'd never heard of *The Wizard of Oz*. And while I'm at it, I wish I'd never heard of Miss Carnine, or spring plays, or Toto—that flea trap of Amy's tried to bite me yesterday. And come to think of it, I wish I'd never heard of *me*."

"Don't you think you're getting a little carried away, Jill?"

I sighed. "I guess so. I'm sorry, Wendy. But I'm so disappointed; what fun is it to be Dorothy if my very own family isn't there to see me?"

"My mom and dad and brother will be there," Wendy pointed out. "And they'll be applauding for you, just as much as they will for me. Maybe you can kind of adopt them for one night."

I gave her shoulder a little punch. "You're a good friend, Wendy," I said. "I just hope I won't forget these lines!"

"Could you learn them any better if your mom was going to be there on Friday?" Wendy asked.

I stared at her. "What a dumb question!" I exclaimed. "What difference would that make?"

"Well, you've been acting as if it would make a *big* difference," Wendy pointed out. "As if you had to have your mom there, or you couldn't do a thing. And that's not true, Jill. You know it isn't. You can do this part whether your mom's at the play or not."

"Funny," I told her. "My mom said the same thing."

Wendy laughed. "Let's do our math, and

then we can try that last scene again. Maybe all you need is to get away from it for a little while."

"Mmmmm," I said. "Maybe."

But as I opened my book to the chapter on fractions—yuck!—I knew that it was going to take more than that to make me a halfway decent Dorothy.

It was going to take a miracle.

Then, somehow, it was the day before the play, and we were getting ready for the dress rehearsal, which was going to last all afternoon. In the back of my mind, I was still afraid I'd forget every line in the play and miss my dance steps, even though I knew I had them pretty well learned by now. And when I thought about standing up there and singing, there seemed to be a big, tough wad of cotton right in the back of my throat. How did I get myself into this, anyway? I wondered, taking my place on the stage for the first scene.

And the butterflies in my stomach seemed to get worse and worse as the rehearsal went on. I kept thinking about Mom, and everyone from Auntie Em to the Cowardly Lion seemed to have her face. A couple of times, as I stood backstage waiting to make an entrance, I had to swallow hard to keep the tears from overflowing. But nobody said anything, so I guessed I was managing to hide it pretty well. Even Miss Carnine went out of her way to tell me she liked the way I sounded in my first solo.

I would have been all right, too, if I hadn't had to say that corny line right before the end: "There's no place like home."

Suddenly, as I was saying that line, I thought about the way things had been around *our* home lately, and all my feelings flooded in like a river when the dam breaks. Before I even knew what happened, I was running offstage with hot tears streaming down my face, leaving the Wizard and the Tin Man and the Scarecrow standing there with their mouths wide open.

Backstage, I leaned against a piece of scenery, breathing in the smell of paint, and crying so hard I couldn't catch my breath. What had made me think I could go through with this, anyway? What had even made me think I *wanted* to?

"Jill?" It was Miss Carnine's soft voice, right behind me. Reaching over my shoulder, she pushed a tissue into my hand, and I dabbed at my eyes, although that was a little like trying to dry up the Mississippi River with a bath towel. "Jill, honey, please—turn around and look at me. Would you like to talk for a minute?"

Still crying, I turned around, and Miss Carnine wrapped both arms around my shoulders. It felt good, so I just leaned against her, smelling her flowery perfume and letting my tears soak her fluffy pink sweater.

"Jill," she said quietly. "I know what's happening. Wendy was worried about you, and she came to talk to me a few days ago. I know your mother won't be at the play."

"Wendy shouldn't have told you that." I sighed, but I was too miserable to get mad. "That's private stuff."

"I haven't told another soul, and I won't," she promised. "But now I think I know why you've been so nervous and upset lately."

I nodded, but without lifting my head from her shoulder. "It hurts that Mom won't be there," I said. "After all this work, too.

How can I go on that stage if there's no one here to even see me?"

"Jill," Miss Carnine said, patting my arm. "Honey, in the long run, you can't lean on other people. No one can go up on that stage with you tomorrow night, and this performance is more than just a show for everyone's parents. You have to learn to rely on yourself. You have to be strong enough to know that you can do anything—*anything*—you really want to do, even if there's no one to help you or to praise you for your accomplishments. That's what growing up is all about."

I thought about it. "Well," I said, "it isn't going to be easy, Miss Carnine."

"That's another part of growing up." She laughed. "Doing things even when they aren't easy. But I know you can. And there's one other thing I know, too, Jill; I've met your mother, and I know that she loves you very much. She's very proud of you, too."

I looked up at her. "Really?" I sniffed. "How do you know that?"

She smiled and used her finger to brush a tear from my cheek. "She told me so," she said. "She told me so herself."

"Oh." I hiccupped.

"It's true." She swiveled me around so I was facing the stage. "We have a show to rehearse, Jill. Ready to go back in there?"

I tried a smile. "I guess," I said.

"Atta girl." She pushed me back toward the stage. "Now you go out there and knock 'em dead. You're going to be the best Dorothy anyone ever saw!"

"I'll try, Miss Carnine," I said, and blew my nose and scrubbed the last tears from my face. "Okay, guys! Where were we? Dorothy's back!"

And, for the rest of the rehearsal, I almost managed to forget that things weren't so perfect in the wonderful land of Oz.

CHAPTER ELEVEN

A Star Is Born

The day of the play. I had looked forward to today for so long, and now I was too nervous to enjoy it. I couldn't spell "cat" or add 2 + 2 or even eat my lunch. And it didn't help any that Wendy kept asking me if I was okay. To top it all off, I had a headache from not sleeping all night. Even the "Good Luck" card my mom had tucked into my lunchbox couldn't kill the butterflies in my stomach.

Then, sometime during the afternoon, I decided that the best thing for me to do was to give such a great performance that Mom and Jessica would have to be proud of me, even if they couldn't be in the audience. Maybe there'd be a TV reporter there to film the play, I daydreamed. Or a newspaper photographer. And whoever it was would be so impressed by the brilliant young actress playing Dorothy that they'd do a special story about me. "A STAR IS BORN"—I could see the headlines in tomorrow morning's paper, in big black letters three inches high. The phone would start ringing at sunup, with talent scouts from Hollywood and magazine editors and people begging me to let them be president of the first Jill Armstrong International Fan Club.

Miss Carnine was right; I could do it. I didn't need anyone's help to be a star.

I decided I couldn't wait for the curtain to open.

Because Mom and Jessica had to leave right after school to get to Lake of the Ozarks for the pageant, I ate supper at Wendy's house. Wendy's mom had fixed all my favorite things, like corn on the cob and baked beans and hamburgers, but I only managed to swallow a bite or two. Then her dad drove us to the school, promising that the whole family would be back later for the play.

Lucky Wendy, I thought.

Now I pushed and jostled and shoved with a whole room full of sixth graders, standing in front of the long mirrors as we put on our stage makeup, which was sticky and goopy and smelled like Play-Doh.

"Hey!" the Cowardly Lion yelled, off to my left. "Get off my tail! Somebody's standing on my tail!"

"I can't find my wand!" the Good Witch wailed. "Has anyone seen my wand?"

"Can I borrow your mascara?"

"Miss Carnine, help—my zipper won't zip!"

"Hey, Amy, you'd better get your dog outside. He just threw up on a pile of programs!"

"Heh-heh-heh!"—that was from the Wicked Witch of the West, naturally.

It was a complete nuthouse, and any other time I would have thought it was exciting. But as I stood there in the blue-and-white checked dress that Mom had made, with my hair in braids, the way Jessica had taught me to fix it, and a lot of blue goop on my eyelids, I didn't feel much of anything except sick.

This was my night. My big night. And there was no one out front for me—no one to cheer me on, except maybe Wendy's parents. This wasn't going to be any fun at all.

I almost wished I had never heard of *The Wizard of Oz*.

Nothing felt real as the curtain rose for the first scene of the play. All through the first part, as I argued with Auntie Em and tried to rescue my poor little dog from the mean old lady, it was just as if everything were happening in a dream. I hardly even saw the audience, or heard the music, or felt the hot glow of the spotlight. The only part that seemed real was the part where Dorothy runs away. I couldn't help thinking that I knew just how Dorothy felt.

Then it was time for my first solo. Poor little Dorothy, wandering around Kansas, with a tornado on the way, alone, rejected, misunderstood. All of a sudden the music starts and she sings about dreams and rainbows. It always makes me want to cry.

I faced the audience, heard Miss Carnine's piano ripple into the introduction, opened my mouth to sing—and almost choked on the first words. Way back near the rear of the auditorium, sitting in the very last row—was I seeing wrong? Could it be—could it possibly be? My heart beat fast as Miss Carnine came to the end of the introduction. No, it couldn't be. But it was. I knew it was. It was Mom and Jessica. They had come to the play after all. I didn't have time to wonder how or why. It was time to sing. But I did feel a big smile tugging at the corners of my mouth as the song came out, better than I had ever sung it before.

And, from the last row, my mother smiled back at me.

CHAPTER TWELVE

There's No Place Like Home

I hardly remember anything about the rest of the play, except that I was happy, maybe happier than I'd ever been before in my whole life. Oh, yeah—I do remember coming out in front of the curtain to take a lot of bows, and getting a little bouquet of pink roses from Miss Carnine. But I hardly even saw the flowers, because I was looking at the back row, where my mother and Jessica were clapping their hands off, with grins all over their faces.

"Wow!" The minute we were offstage,

Wendy threw her arms around my neck. "They came! See, I told you everything would be okay!"

I smiled a dopey smile. "It's better than okay," I said. "Everything is great!" And I rushed to take off my makeup so I could find Mom and Jessica. They were waiting for me just outside the dressing room door. Mom saw me coming and hurried toward me, her arms open wide. I ran straight into her hug, not even caring if all the other kids were watching.

"Mom," I whispered. "Mom, I'm so glad you were there."

"I couldn't have missed it," she said.

Jessica stepped forward, pushing a bouquet of red carnations into my arms. "Here," she said. "For you, because I'm so proud of you."

"Jessica!" I buried my nose in the flowers. "You didn't have to do that."

She hung her head. "It's okay," she said. "They're just the flowers I was supposed to carry in the pageant. We didn't have time to stop by the florist's before we came here, so I'm giving you my flowers instead."

"But what happened?" I asked. "What

about the pageant? Why aren't you there?"

"We were actually on our way," Mom explained. "In fact, we were almost half-way there, and I pulled off the freeway to put gas in the car at one of those big truck stops. All of a sudden we looked at each other, and I knew we were both thinking the same thing. And that was when Jessica said—"

"*Jessica?*" I interrupted.

Mom smiled. "She said, 'We still have time to make the play, Mom.' And I said, 'Are you sure?' But we both agreed, there was no place we'd rather be. So I turned the car around and came back, just as fast as I could drive."

"You did that—for me?" I had trouble get-ting the words out, with the big lump in my throat.

"We missed a few minutes, but we were in time for your big solo," Jessica said. "You did a great job, too, Jill. I knew you would."

I was still puzzled. "I can't believe it," I said. "You mean, you actually volunteered to miss the pageant? I thought it meant so much to you!"

Jessica grinned kind of an embarrassed-looking grin. "It's not like you're some stray dog or something," she mumbled. "You're my *sister*, Jill. I—I know I'm a pain sometimes. And I guess you're right that I can hog all the attention, too. But I don't mean to. I really did want to see your play. And it's like you said—there'll be other pageants."

"That goes for me, too," Mom put in softly. "I'm proud of my girls tonight—both of them."

"Aw, come on," I protested. "Things are starting to get pretty mushy around here."

"You're right." Mom laughed. "Anyway, don't you have a cast party to go to? Come on, I'll drop you and Wendy off at the pizza parlor. We can talk later."

I turned to go back to the dressing room. But then something made me turn around again.

"Mom? Jessica?" I said. "Thanks. Thanks a lot."

Jessica smiled, and Mom gave me a thumbs-up sign as I pushed open the dressing room door.

"Wendy?" I called. "Are you still in there?

Get a move on, or there's not going to be any pizza left!"

"Yay, Jill!"
"Way to go, Dorothy!"
"You were great!"
The second Wendy and I stepped through the front door of the pizza parlor, I was surrounded by all my friends, who were laughing and waving pizza in my face.

"Here!" Rachel called from a big table by the wall. "We saved you guys places! Get over here while the pizza's hot!"

We spent the next hour wolfing down pizza and playing video games and going over every single second of the play again and again.

"Did you see Peaches when the Wicked Witch grabbed him?" Amy asked. "I thought he was going to bite her for sure!"

"And did you hear the way everyone applauded when we Munchkins did our big dance?" John Paul wanted to know. "We stopped the whole show!"

"What about the scenery?" I said, glancing at Wendy. "It was gorgeous!"

"And I thought the way Jill sang was just beautiful," Wendy pointed out loyally. "My mom said it even made her cry."

I looked up to see Miss Carnine smiling at me across the table. "You know," she said softly, "Jill promised me she was going to be the best Dorothy ever. And I think she did it, too."

I could feel my face turning pink. And, at the same time, I could feel a warm, happy glow that seemed to start right in my middle and spread out to every finger and toe.

"Well," I said modestly, "I guess I wasn't too bad. Pass the cheese, please, Wendy."

"I thought the best part was the way you said, 'There's no place like home,' at the end," Stephanie said. "You sounded like you really meant it."

"Thanks," I said. "I did mean it. But now I've decided that even though there's no place like home, it's important to depend on yourself. You can't be a little kid and lean on other people your whole life. Right, Miss Carnine?"

Miss Carnine winked at me. "Right, Dorothy," she said. "I wonder if the real Dorothy ever figured that out?"

"Hey!" Stuart yelled. "Someone just spilled Coke all over my new sweater! Cut it out, you guys!"

Then we were back to licking ice cream cones and making gross slurpy noises with our drinking straws. But that warm, good feeling was still there, deep down inside of me. And the best part was, I knew I had earned it—all by myself.

"Thanks, Wendy," I murmured sleepily, as the two of us stood inside the door of the pizza parlor, waiting for Mom and Jessica to pick us up.

"What for?" She yawned. She sounded tired, too.

"Just for—you know." I was embarrassed, but I had to say it. "Just for being my friend, even when I act like a jerk."

She laughed. "Forget it," she said. "What are friends for? Anyway, everything turned out okay, didn't it? I knew it would."

"I still can't get over it," I marveled, shaking my head. "I mean, the way Mom and Jessica drove all the way back here to see my play. I can't believe they'd do that for me—Jessica especially."

"I can," Wendy informed me. "Your mom's really a pretty neat lady. And you may not be able to see it yourself, but Jessica—well, Jessica's special, too."

I grinned at her. "Hmmm," I joked. "Must run in the family."

"There's your mom!" Wendy exclaimed, waving. "Come on, Jill; let's run!"

And the two of us dashed for the parking lot, where my mother and little sister were waiting for us.

After all, there really is no place like home.

About the Author

Constance Hiser was born in Joplin, Missouri, and received her degree in literature from Missouri Southern State College. She lives in Webb City, Missouri, with her husband and two children. Her other books include *Critter Sitters*, *Dog on Third Base*, *Ghosts in Fourth Grade*, and *No Bean Sprouts, Please!*, all available from Minstrel Books.

R·L·STINE'S

GHOSTS of FEAR STREET ®

1 HIDE AND SHRIEK 52941-2/$3.99
2 WHO'S BEEN SLEEPING IN MY GRAVE? 52942-0/$3.99
3 THE ATTACK OF THE AQUA APES 52943-9/$3.99
4 NIGHTMARE IN 3-D 52944-7/$3.99
5 STAY AWAY FROM THE TREE HOUSE 52945-5/$3.99
6 EYE OF THE FORTUNETELLER 52946-3/$3.99
7 FRIGHT KNIGHT 52947-1/$3.99
8 THE OOZE 52948-X/$3.99
9 REVENGE OF THE SHADOW PEOPLE 52949-8/$3.99
10 THE BUGMAN LIVES! 52950-1/$3.99
11 THE BOY WHO ATE FEAR STREET 00183-3/$3.99
12 NIGHT OF THE WERECAT 00184-1/$3.99
13 HOW TO BE A VAMPIRE 00185-X/$3.99
14 BODY SWITCHERS FROM OUTER SPACE 00186-8/$3.99
15 FRIGHT CHRISTMAS 00187-6/$3.99